# Monica's
# Revenge

# MONICA'S REVENGE

PATRICIA MURPHY

PARTRIDGE
A Penguin Random House Company

**To order additional copies of this book, contact**
Toll Free 800 101 2657 (Singapore)
Toll Free 1 800 81 7340 (Malaysia)
orders.singapore@partridgepublishing.com

www.partridgepublishing.com/singapore

# CHAPTER 1

# The New Gang

Every day Monica goes for a ride. She loves getting away from her father and his nagging. One morning on her usual ride she found a campsite with a very large black man sitting by his fire, enjoying his morning coffee. "Oh, that smells good. Do you have enough for two?" Monica asked as she got close to him.

Without looking to see who it was, he said, "Come, there is enough for both of us, Monica."

She was surprised to find out he knew her. "Um, who are you?" she asked. That is when he turned around. "Sammy, you old bugger, I was told you were dead."

"And I was told the same thing about you." After all the hugging and patting each other on the back, they sat there for most of the day, planning their next move.

"Sammy, I will leave everything up to you, and I will meet you back here in two days," Monica said, and then she left.

By the time Monica got back to her father's home, it was very late. Her father had finished supper and was sitting in the den when Monica came in. "You're late. The cook left some supper on the kitchen table for you."

"Yeah, Pa, but I am not hungry." With that, she went straight to her room.

The next day she was up early and went out to the stables. She needed to get away from her father; she could not stand his nagging. Monica needed to find a place of her own. There was a small cottage close to town that she knew about, and this would be the ideal place to set up right under their noses.

No one had lived in the cottage for years, so it was up for grabs. Monica soon made it livable, and the townspeople were none the wiser.

The next day Monica met Sammy at the arranged meeting place. When she got there, there were three others with him: one woman and two men. The woman was very tall, and she had long black hair braided down her back. She wore black jeans that were tucked in her high boots, and around her black shirt she had a gun strapped down like a gunfighter would. Monica wanted to see just what this woman could do, but that would have to wait. One of the men had blue eyes and blond hair, and he looked like he would not harm a flee, but that was to be seen. The other one did not seem to care about much—that was plain to see. His clothes were not much to look at, and his hair had not seen a comb in months.

Monica told Sammy where she was living now and to have everyone there tonight. That night Monica laid out her plan for a raid on a small wagon train.

"Shana, you take care of the wagon master. We will handle the rest. Now get some rest. We leave at daybreak."

Chad was sitting back in his chair at the office, thinking that it had been very quiet around town. His deputy, Ben, came in. "Hey, Chad, it's so quiet around here. Why don't you take that holiday you have wanted to take."

"Yeah, you're right. I might just do that. You can handle things here for a while."

The next day Chad was up and gone before the sun came up. He wanted to get to Jake's place before dark, and it was a very long ways away.

Monica and her gang were out waiting for the wagon train to come. Nigel was down the track a bit. As soon as he saw the wagon train, he would signal by mirror to Monica.

It was about noon when the wagon train came into view, and Nigel signaled to Monica. But she was not the only one who saw the flash of the mirror.

Chad was in the area, and he saw the flash. *What the bloody hell was that?* He sat on his horse and looked around, and as he did not see anything else suspicious, he went on his way. The sun was going down when he got to Jake's place.

Monica and her gang were all over the wagons. Shana found the wagon master, jumped from her horse to his, and then put a very sharp knife to his throat. "Don't move, and I might let you live. What is your name?"

"I am Mark. What do you want? We don't have anything of great value."

"My boss will be the judge of that. Now stop wriggling."

Rodney got up into one of the wagons and found a strongbox hidden behind some sacks of flower. *Well, what do we have here?* he thought to himself. The box had a padlock on it, but that was not going to stop him. With one hard hit with the butt of his gun, he soon had that box open. What he found was a lot of cash, maybe their life savings. That was not enough for Rodney. He tipped over a lantern, lit a match, and set fire to the wagon. He did not know that Mr. Mathews was under the wagon, and he could not get out. The fire took hold very fast.

Monica called out, "Come on, you lot. Let's get the hell out of here."

Shana hit the wagon master over the head with her gun and then just left him.

When they all got back to the house, they had to put all of their takings on the kitchen table. Monica had a look at what they got. "Mmm ... not very good, but we should do better next time." Sammy knew that Monica already had a plan in mind.

Jake met Chad at the door. "Hi, Chad, what brings you all the way out here?"

"Oh, old pal, I hear you had good trout fishing around here."

"Um, yeah. Nothing to do in town, eh?"

"Nope, it is quieter than a graveyard."

"Well, maybe I can put someone in charge. I could do with a few days off."

Very early the next day, they had packed all they needed for a few days of good fishing.

Monica and her men just sat around the house, doing nothing. Sammy had just gotten back from doing the marketing.

"Monica, that wagon train you raided a few days ago—the wagon master just came into town looking for the sheriff."

"Oh, did he? Well, they don't know it was us, and the sheriff has gone fishing." She walked away, laughing.

Chad and Jake had a good time fishing, but now it was time to get back to work. They had just gotten back to Jake's place and found the deputy waiting for them.

"Come quick, there is trouble in town," the deputy said, walking back and forth. He looked very shaken.

"Calm down, Deputy, and tell me just what is going on in town." Chad sat the deputy down on the porch. Then the deputy told Chad all about the raid on the wagon train. "Okay, okay, take it easy. Jake, I would like you in on this. It sounds like—"

"Yes, I know Monica, but she is dead," Jake butted in.

At the sheriff's office, the wagon master was waiting. "Hi, are you the sheriff? I have been waiting a long time to see you."

"Yes, my name is Chad. What is yours, and what do you want?" Chad was in no mood for niceness.

"I am Mark. I brought the wagon train in … what was left of it."

"Ah, yes, my deputy told me all about the trouble you and your friends had. I am doing all I can right now."

"I understand this, Sheriff, but I want to help."

"Ah, that is all well and good, but you had better leave it up to those who know what they are doing."

"But, Sheriff—"

"No 'buts,'" Chad interrupted Mark.

While she was busy with the first raid Monica and her gang did, she was planning her next move. She knew that the payroll for the rail workers was due to come in very soon. As soon as she knew it was time, she had her gang out there waiting for it. She had good cover, so the guards on the train could not see her or her gang. As soon as the train had passed, they boarded the train at the back. They walked through the train to get to the baggage car. As usual, Rodney had an eye on the rear to make sure no one came up behind them.

Mark walked out of the office and decided to take the law into his own hands. Chad was talking to Jake when Mark left and did not see him go. "Chad, you know that Mark could identify the gang that raided the wagon train," Jake reminded him.

"Ah, yes, you are right, pal. Where did he go? I want to talk to him."

Chad and Jake found Mark in his room, packing.

"And where do you think you are going?" Chad asked.

"It is none of your business, so back off."

"If you think you are going out there to take the law into your own hands, think again, pal," Chad told him.

"I am not your pal, so back off."

With that, Mark took a swing at Chad and missed.

Jake stepped into the room to try to get Mark to see sense. "Come on, Mark, we need you to help us. You know what they look like."

Mark sat on the end of the bed with his head in his hands. "All right, I will help you. That's about all I am good for."

Chad put his hand on Mark's shoulder. "Don't be so hard on yourself. You did get the wagons into town. That counts for something."

In the baggage car, Monica came up on one of the guards and let him have it over the head with the butt of her gun. The other one swung round and was going to shoot Monica, but Shana was so fast with her knife, it hit the guard in the heart, and he dropped like a rock to the floor.

Nigel had the horses ready to go once the money was loaded. But there was someone they did not count on. One of the passengers got off the train and started to shoot at Nigel. He ducked behind his horse and shot back. Shana put her head around the door of the baggage car, and as quick as lightning, her knife flew through the air and hit the man in the arm. Then the man grabbed his arm and went back on the train.

Monica and her gang returned to the house. Sammy had a hot bath waiting for Monica. She loved to relax this way after a raid.

Chad and his men were out where the wagon train was raided. Mark told them that they came out of the hills very fast, and there was nothing they could do to defend themselves. Mark showed them what was left of Mr. Matthews's wagon and where they buried him.

They took a good look around. "By the looks of the tracks there were four horses. Mark, can you tell us a little more about them?"

"Yes, there were two women and two men. They were led by a Spanish woman. She is the one that gave all the orders."

Both Chad and Jake just looked at each other. They knew who it was they were looking for. But as far as they knew, she was dead. Chad and Jake decided to go visit Monica's father to see if he could shed some light on the matter.

Monica told the gang that she would be away for a few days and they could catch up on some work around the house. "Sammy, I want you to come with me," Monica said.

They set out the next day. The gang did not know just what to make of it.

When they got clear of the house, Sammy asked, "Now, Monica, can you let me in on the big secret?"

"Ah, my good friend, we are going to see the Indians and talk to the chief."

"Um … the last time you talked to the chief things did not go so well. What makes you think it will this time?"

"I just hope it will, but just in case it does not go the way I want it to, be ready to get out of there fast."

"Will do."

The house of Monica's father, Mr. Nick Carlo, was a good way off. They did not need Mark there, so they told him to wait for them back in town. Chad and Jake were greeted at the front gate by the foreman.

"Tell Senior Carlo that the sheriff and friend would like a word with him."

"You had better come up to the sitting room."

It did not take long before Mr. Carlo came in to see them. "Gentlemen, what can I do for you?"

"Senior Carlo, it is about your daughter, Monica."

"Ah, no, no, you don't understand. I have not seen my daughter for many years. I do not know if she is living or dead." Nick was not about to turn his only child into the law, no matter what she had done.

While Chad was talking to Nick, Jake had a careful look around to see if he could see any sign of Monica having been there.

# CHAPTER 2

# The Hunt for Monica

Chad and Jake left Nick's house. "Well, Jake, did you see anything that said she was there?"

"There was a lady's sun hat and scarf hanging on the hall stand."

"Good, that is all we need. Now, we can start hunting her down again, and this time she will go straight to prison."

Mark was on his way back to town when he came across a woman sitting near the lake, reading a book. From where he was he could not see her face. But when he got close he could see her. He knew he had seen her somewhere but could not remember.

"Hi, how are you? I am Mark."

Shana put the book down. Shielding her eyes from the sun, she said, "Oh, I am Shana, but I was just about to leave." She knew who he was and tried to get away very fast.

"Don't let me scare you off."

"No, I must go." With that, she leaped onto her horse and took off fast.

Monica and Sammy were greeted by two big braves at the edge of the Indian camp. They pointed spears at them and made them move very slowly into the camp.

The chief knew they were coming, so he stayed in his tepee. Monica and Sammy were taken to another tepee, and their hands were bound with rope.

"Sammy, it looks like I have to do a lot of fast talking if we get the chance."

"Yes, I would think so—very fast, if we are to get out of this one."

After a while the chief came to see them. "Well, Monica, what is it that you want?"

"I have come to make friends with you. I know I did the wrong thing by you and your people, and I am sorry. Really sorry. Is there any way I can make it up to you?" Monica begged the chief.

"Maybe, but you will have to show that you mean it. I will think on it. Come back in two moons." With that, the chief left the tepee and told a brave to let them go.

It was getting late, so Chad and Jake decided to make camp for the night. As Monica and Sammy were in the same area, they too stopped for the night. Sammy started up a fire, and Monica kicked it out.

"Hey, what is the big idea? I want coffee, and I am cold."

"Take a look down there through the trees. See that yellow glow? That is another fire. I don't want anyone to know we are here."

Monica sat close to Sammy all night. It was bitterly cold. As soon as it got light, they headed for home and a warm fire.

Mark got back to town and sat in the hotel room, trying to think about where he had seen her before. But nothing was coming forward. He was involved in his thoughts and did not see Nigel and Rodney walk into the bar. But they saw him and did a quick about-face.

"That was close, pal," Nigel said.

"Yeah, let's get the hell out of here." Rodney started to move fast. No matter how hard they searched, it seemed like she had covered her tracks.

Chad and Jake had to wait till she made her next move and hope to pick up her trail then.

It was time Jake got back to his ranch. There was work he had to see to. "Sorry, I have to get back to the ranch. It won't run itself," Jake said to Chad.

"That's okay, pal. I understand. We are just chasing our tails." Chad slapped Jake on the back.

When Jake came to where he had to go so he could get back to his ranch, he said, "Well, pal, this is where I leave you. Don't hesitate to send a message and I will be there."

"Thanks, buddy, I will. We need to put that bitch behind bars for the last time."

Monica went straight to her room for a hot bath. Sammy had the same idea. It was so good to be back safe.

Shana was coming from a room upstairs in the hotel, and Mark was going up. They met on the bottom of the stairs. "I know you, but I can't for the life of me remember from where," Mark remarked.

"Oh, it will come to you." Shana kept on walking. Now there were two things that set him to thinking. *What the hell was she doing up there?* he thought to himself as he went up to his room. He was not thinking about whether or not she had set a trap for him. When he got to the door of his room, he could see that someone was in there. The door was not closed right. Suddenly it dawned on him that she was in his room. He put his hand on the doorknob and then realized he had seen what a shotgun can do.

Chad had just gotten to town. It was very late, and he had just fallen into bed when he heard someone banging on the door. He called out, "This had better be a case of life or death or you are dead." Chad did not know how close he was to that statement.

When he opened the door, a very excited little man was standing there. "Come quick, there's a bomb in the room." The little man ran back to the hotel, with Chad right behind him.

"Mark, what the devil is going on here?"

"Um … nothing much. I just think my room has been booby-trapped."

"How?"

"The shotgun-tied-to-the-doorknob trick."

"Mmm … okay. I will be back in a minute." Chad was not long, and when he came back he had a long pole in his hand. "Okay, step back." Chad pushed the door open with the long pole. The shotgun went off and blew a hole right through the door of the room opposite them.

"Mark, do you know who did this? Maybe it was set to warn you."

"Or kill me and warn you."

"What do you know about this, Mark?"

"I think we had better finish this over at the office."

When Shana got back home, Monica asked, "Where have you been? Or maybe I should ask, what have you been up to? We heard a loud explosion over at the hotel. Did you have anything to do with that? By the look on your face, I would say you did, and who was the poor bastard that copped it?"

"We will see if he is dumb or not," Shana said as she walked past Monica with a large smile on her face.

"Now, Mark, you can tell me all about what went on at the hotel," Chad demanded.

"Yes, I will. There is something I forgot to tell you and Jake earlier."

"This sounds serious. You had better sit down and fill me in."

Mark told Chad all about Shana, that he had seen her before but could not remember where he had seen her.

"So, we do not have one woman to look for—we have two. Great. Just great. Tell me all you know about this woman. What is her name? What does she look like? Come on, Mark, give me something, anything."

Mark sat there thinking. "Um, she is about six feet six inches tall, always wears black clothes. She looks to be Spanish. She has black hair in a braid down her back. Oh, yes, she always carries a lot of knives. She is very good with them. Dummy me, now I remember where I have seen her before. She was one of the gang that raided the wagons."

"Great, that's all we need, two Spanish females. That one is just as bad as the other," Chad replied.

After Mark left, Chad sent a message to Jake, asking him to meet him at the waterfall.

Chad got to the waterfall first, set up camp, and waited for Jake. It was not long before Jake got there. "Hi, pal, what is the emergency?"

"Sit down. You will need a coffee for this. Sorry, I don't have anything stronger," Chad said as he handed him the coffee.

"One of those kinds of emergencies. I hate that kind."

"Well, buddy, it is like this. We have two Spanish outlaw women to send straight to hell."

"You mean Monica has a backup?" Jake asked.

"Uh-huh, you got it in one"

"Okay, where do we start?" Jake inquired.

"Right here, my friend. We go and talk to the Indians."

"Oh, this keeps on getting better and better," Jake remarked.

Monica and Sammy set out for the Indian camp. They did not know that Jake and Chad were on their way, as well. Chad and Jake were halfway through the tunnel when they heard someone coming. There was a pile of rocks just big enough to hide them and their horses, so they could see who was behind them. Monica and Sammy were walking their horses very slowly. Monica knew that something was not quite right; her sixth sense was not going to let her down. She beckoned Sammy to come close so she could tell him something without anyone overhearing.

Mark was making arrangements to leave town when he heard a woman's voice downstairs. She was talking to two men. Mark thought he knew the woman so he stood near the window so he could hear better. At one time he even peeked out the window. *Yes, it is her, and the two men are her friends,* he thought to himself. Although he could not hear what they were saying, he was going to follow them and see what they were up to.

Monica told Sammy to make a hasty retreat. "Sammy, I think there is someone up ahead, so go back."

Jake and Chad waited for a while. After not hearing any noise for a while, they went on. "Phew, that was close. I don't know who it was or how many there were, but it was close," Chad said.

Monica and Sammy made it to the waterfall entrance. "Sammy, I think the law is up at the front of the tunnel. It is too close for me."

Sammy looked out past the water and could see some soldiers making camp. This meant that they could not leave the tunnel and could not go back in the tunnel. "Monica, we are trapped."

"What the hell are you saying?" She looked out and saw just what he meant. "Great, now we have to stay."

But it was not a good idea to stay too long. Jake and Chad had to come back that way. All they could do was watch and hope the soldiers left before the law got back.

At the hotel, Mark was watching the three outlaws. When they moved, he moved. It was a case of cat and mouse for now. Then Rodney got some hay from the barn and started to stack it up against the hotel wall. "This will make the rats run." Rodney then struck a match and tossed it onto the hay. The building caught on fire very fast. Mark ran inside to warn them. Everyone came running with buckets of water to put the fire out. The three outlaws took off like the scrolled rats they were.

"Ah, Rodney, old bean, that did not work," Nigel snickered.

Rodney did not like being made a fool of, so he hauled off and hit Nigel with all of his might. That sent Nigel backward onto his ass. Nigel got to his feet. "Ah, you shouldn't have done that." Then Nigel swung at Rodney and got him right on the nose.

Shana stepped in between them. "Come on, this is not getting us anywhere. We need to focus on who did dropped us in it. Someone was following us, and I think I know who."

Monica was running out of time fast. She had to get to the chief. He gave her two moons to show him she really cared about the Indians.

"Monica, we could still get to the chief before the law." Sammy said

"Yeah, how?"

"Well, you know, your old house. There is a hidden track behind the house that leads right to the back of the chief's tepee."

"Yes, I forgot about that, but it must be overgrown by now. Do you think you could still find it?"

"Yes. What have we got to lose?"

They packed up a packhorse with all of the goods they were taking to the chief.

Chad and Jake found themselves going the wrong way. "Jake, this does not look like the right way. What do you think?"

"I think you are right, pal."

While Chad and Jake were trying to figure out just where they went wrong, Monica and Sammy were getting close to the chief's tepee.

The fire was finally put out, and there was not much damage done to the building. Shana and her friends were not happy. They were trying to do as much damage to the town as they could.

Maybe it was time to do something to the stables. "I think it is time we made sure that nobody follows us this time," Shana told the men. Mark was in his room when Rodney came up the back to Mark's door very quietly and jammed a wooden chair under the doorknob so hard the door would not open without a lot of force.

After they took care of Mark, they went around the back of the church. Because it was Sunday, they knew there would be a lot of people in the church. Nigel was concerned for the people inside.

"But, Shana, there are people in the church."

"Nigel, orders are orders, and if we do not do what she wants, we better just keep on riding, because she will find us somewhere."

"Okay, just as you say."

Then they lit the bales of hay they had stacked up earlier.

"All right, guys, let's get to the stables and do the same."

Now there were two buildings going up in flames. The deputy could not do much. He helped to get some of the people out of the church.

Other people in the town tried to put the flames out, but it was of no use. The fire had a good hold on the buildings.

Monica and Sammy were almost at the chief's tepee when they hit a snag, stopping them from going any farther for now. This holdup gave Jake and Chad time to get back on the right track.

"This way, Chad. If I remember it right, we should see Monica's old house soon."

"I hope so. I am all but done in," Chad complained.

A landslide had put some very large boulders in their way. This meant that they had to track around them, and it would take longer. Monica was all but done in, but she would not let Sammy know.

"Monica, we will have to go around though the swamp. Do you think you can make it?"

"Sammy, don't worry about me. Just one thing—will we get there before the law?"

"I think so. It has been a long time since I have been this way."

"Okay, let's push on and see what happens."

Monica and Sammy waded through the swamp. Because they had to leave the packhorses, they had to carry all their items themselves.

# CHAPTER 3

# Let the Games Begin

Chad and Jake got to Monica's old house.

An Indian dressed all in white came to the door. "You seek Miss Monica? She does not live here. I am White Cloud Indian doctor," he said.

"We know this, but we are looking for the Indian camp. Can you take us there?"

"Yes, we'll go now." He seemed to want to get rid of Jake and Chad for some reason. White Cloud did not take them straight to the Indian camp. Jake became aware of this when they walked past the same clump of bushes they had passed before.

"Chad, he is taking us in circles. See that clump of bushes? We passed that a while ago."

"Hey, pal, you're right. Good catch." Chad went to White Cloud and asked, "What do you think you are playing, you asshole? We have been going around in circles. You had better get your act together and show us the right way." Chad pulled out his gun and stuck it to the Indian's head. "You understand me?"

"Yes, yes, we go this way." The Indian pointed in the direction they had to go.

Monica and Sammy finally got out of the swamp, and it only took a little while before they could see the Indian camp. "Oh, at last! I thought we were going to die in there."

"No, Monica, I would not let that happen to you." Sammy had some softness in his voice. Monica felt that Sammy had some feelings for her. This touched her deeply. Maybe they were more than good friends.

Mark finally got out of his room and went to help the others. When Shana saw that Mark had gotten out, she and the men left town. After all the fires were out, the deputy went back to the office, and Mark was not far behind him. "Deputy, I want to see Chad when he gets back. I know who is behind all of this."

"Ah, do you? Well, you can tell me. I am in charge for now."

"That's okay. I will wait. Chad will know what to do." Mark went to what was left of the stables. Mark looked up and down the street and found that not only the horses from the stables were gone, but there was not a horse left anywhere. This left everyone stranded, so he had to get some men together and walk to the nearest farm to borrow some horses to go look for their horses.

Monica and Sammy came up to the chief's tepee. "Monica, you came in time. Let us sit and talk."

While they were talking, Sammy took a walk and kept a good eye out for Chad and Jake. But there was no need for that, as the chief always had braves on the lookout.

One brave came running to the camp and said to Sammy, "The law—they are coming."

Sammy went into the tepee and whispered in Monica's ear, "We better get our asses out of here."

Monica stood up. "We must go. The law is right behind us." Monica turned to go.

"Stop. We will help you." The chief signaled to one of the braves. "Take these two, and hide them well. The law must not know they are here."

When Chad and Jake arrived at the camp, they were flanked by some braves with very pointy spears. They were taken to the chief. "What does the law want here in Indian camp?"

Chad moved away from the spears a bit. "We are looking for a man and a woman. They are wanted by the law."

"Why do you think they are here? We do not have bad people here."

"These people were good friends of the Indians."

"Ah, you mean bad Monica. She is not welcome here anymore. You can look if you want."

Chad and Jake searched the camp and came up empty.

The chief said, "Now you must go. Leave now." He pointed in the direction they had to go. This took them back to the tunnel.

Shana and the men were camped near the waterfall.

Chad and Jake went slowly to the tunnel. "Jake, I think the chief was hiding something or someone. What was your take on the whole thing?"

"I think you are right, pal, but what can we do? We can't sit around here all day. I have a ranch to run."

"No, but I can set a couple of men to watch the entrance to the tunnel and send a message if anyone shows."

"I guess that will have to do. Let me know what happens."

But things changed all of a sudden. When they got to the entrance of the tunnel, they did not expect to see anyone.

Mark and some of the townsmen came back with all of the horses. Now Mark could go find Shana and the gang.

The water coming down shielded Jake and Chad from Shana's view. Chad whispered to Jake, "There is someone out there. We must be quiet. We don't want to frighten them or give away the secret of the tunnel."

Monica and Sammy were brought out of hiding. "Too late to go. You stay the night. Leave at sunup." The chief left.

Mark did not know just which way they went, and it was getting late, so they settled down for the night. The next day Mark woke to find an Indian sitting near him with a fire going and coffee on the boil. Mark did not know just what to make of this. Then the Indian said, "I am friend. I fix fire for you. I am Chad's friend too. I will take you to him."

"Thank you. What do they call you?"

"I am called Fighting Bear."

Shana felt that it was time to go. They did not stay in any one place too long. "Hey, guys, let's get out of here. I know another place we can go. We need to keep on the move until we meet up with Monica."

"Where the hell is she?" Rodney growled.

"I don't know. Just keep moving!" Shana shouted.

Chad and Jake saw that Shana had moved on, so they went too. "Um, Jake, are you on your way back home now?"

"Yes, pal, let me know if you want me to help."

"Will do. See ya."

Back at the office, Chad told the deputy and another man to go up to the waterfall and keep watch.

Fighting Bear got Mark to the waterfall. "See the water? You go into it."

"You mean go through the water?"

"Not in water, back of water."

"Oh, I see. There is a tunnel at the back of the water."

"You go."

Mark went to the waterfall and found that he could go behind the water into a tunnel. What he did not know was he had been led into a trap. As soon as he got halfway into the tunnel, he was met by three other Indians with bows and arrows. He knew what this was about, so he did what they wanted him to do.

The Indians took him to the chief. Monica and Sammy were standing next to the chief. The braves pushed Mark to his knees. "Ah, white eyes, I don't know this one." The chief looked at Monica, as if to ask if she knew him. Monica shook her head to say no, and Sammy did the same. "Then he dies." Then the chief ordered some of the braves to take him away.

The next day when Monica and Sammy were leaving, they saw what was left of Mark. Half of him was hanging from one sapling, and half was hanging from another. "Keep walking, Sammy, or this might happen to us. I have never seen the chief this way before."

Monica was glad to get out of there in one piece. She hoped she would never have to go back there.

By this time Shana and the two men had gotten to what was left of the old trading post.

Chad thought he would have a talk with Mark, but when he got to Mark's room, he was not there. All that was there was a badly mangled door. Chad found the hotel manager in the lobby. "Hey, Mike, don't you care about the hotel?"

"What in the hell are you going on about, Sheriff?"

"The room upstairs—one of the doors is busted, and where is Mr. Witherspoon?"

"How should I know? People come and go all the time around here. If you don't have any more questions, I will get on and get that door fixed."

Chad had asked all around town, but no one had seen or heard from him for days.

Sammy and Monica arrived home at last. "Look, Sammy, it looks like our friends had a ball carrying out my orders. Thank god something has gone as I wanted." Monica went inside only to find that her fledglings were not at home.

Chad was at a loss. He did not know where to go from here. He had to get away to clear his head, with Mark missing and half of his town burned down. So he packed up his horse and took off. He did not know how long he would be.

Jake had the same idea. He could not shake the feeling that something was not right. This was very strange, because as luck would have it, he wound up in the same place as Chad did.

"Well, great minds think alike," Jake said.

Chad was surprised to see Jake there. "What are you doing here, pal?"

"I had a bad feeling about things."

"Yes, I felt the same way. Nothing fits. The town's in ashes—well, most of it anyway."

While Chad was out of town, Monica thought this was a good time to start again. She knew that there was a gold shipment going out on the midday stage tomorrow. Monica had to find Shana. First, she was going to need help on this one. Sammy went out to look for the men and Shana. He was getting tired, so he stopped for a rest at the old trading post.

He was making himself some coffee when he heard someone moving about in the back. He was in no mood to mess around, so he just took his gun and fired a shot into the air. "Come out, whoever you are, or I will shoot, and this time I won't miss."

Shana knew the voice, so she called out, "Sammy, it is us. Don't shoot. We are coming out."

"You better get your sorry ass back to town. Monica needs you."

"Keep your shirt on. We will leave at first light." Shana settled down for a good night's sleep. Nigel and Rodney both thought she was very cool to be able to sleep like that.

Chad and Jake both decided to call it a day and camp for the night. "You know, Chad, I think I would like to check the tunnel and then look further around the Indian camp."

"Ah, yeah, I think you are right. I don't know what we will find, if anything, but it is worth a go," Chad agreed.

Sammy and the others were on their way back to the cottage, where Monica was waiting. Monica had gotten dressed like a woman in mourning clothes, with the big black veil over her hat and all. "Come on, you lot, we have work to do. It is almost midday." Monica sent Shana and the two men out to get ready for the coach to pass their way. She boarded the coach as a widow.

Chad and Jake had just gotten to the tunnel. The deputy was still there with one other man. "Deputy, you and your friend can go back to town now. And stay alert. You don't know what might happen."

Chad and Jake went into the tunnel and very quietly out to the Indian camp. They were lucky there were no braves watching the exit. It was not long before they saw body parts still hanging on saplings. "Jake, look here. This must be what is left of Mark."

"Yeah, what a way to go. I have never seen this happen here before. I have heard about it but have never seen it," Jake remarked.

"Neither have I. The chief must be madder than a cut snake. This is a warning that he will kill at the drop of a hat."

# CHAPTER 4

# It's War

The Indians were on a knife's edge and would start a war at any time. Jake and Chad thought that Mark deserved to have a proper burial, so they started to take his remains down, when one of the Indian braves came screaming at them. This yelling brought some more braves and the chief. "You leave him alone. He stays as a warning to others."

"But, Chief, he should be buried. You can't leave him up there. It is not right," Chad told him in no uncertain terms. "You go now, or you will suffer the same fate. Now go."

"Chad, there is nothing we can do here. We best leave." Jake tugged on Chad's shirt.

"Jake, I cannot just leave him there. It is not right."

"We must. We don't want to start a war."

With that, they left.

The coach with Monica was just coming around the bend in the road. This was where they had to stop, because a large tree had fallen across the road. Shana and her men were waiting with their guns drawn. "This is a holdup. Throw down the strongbox," Rodney yelled.

Monica pulled out a small gun and poked it at the side of the passenger next to her. "Move over to the other seat, honey. But before you do, give me all of your valuables." Then she turned the gun on the other passengers. "Come on, don't be shy. Hand them over, all of it, the wallet, to Mr.—"

But the male passenger was not going to give up without a fight. He had a small gun himself, and he pulled it out. "No, you drop your gun, or I will shoot you."

But Monica shot first. The bullet hit the man right in the middle of his forehead. Monica then helped herself to his wallet.

Monica jumped out of the coach. "Okay, let's ride, people." There were only two people left alive, and those were the two ladies in the coach. Shana's knife had found its way to the heart of the driver, and it took only one shot to the head of the guard to silence him.

Monica and her gang were back at home before anyone knew what had happened.

Chad and Jake came into town about one hour after Monica did. At the office Jake and Chad just fell into their chairs. "I don't know what to do now. I feel bad about leaving that poor man back at the Indian camp." Chad put his face in his hands.

Jake walked over to Chad and put his hand on his shoulder. "I know just how you feel, because that is the same way I feel. But the best thing we can do is concentrate on what we have to do now."

Suddenly two women burst into the office. They were dirty dusty and tied Jake sat them down, and Chad gave them some water. "Ladies, can you tell me what happened to you and your friend?"

"First, Sheriff, my name is Millie Parkinson, and this is my friend Nancy Bola. We were on the stagecoach that left town at midday. Not long out of town, we were set upon by some awful thugs. They robbed us and killed the men. We did not know how to drive the coach, so we had to walk back here."

Jake took the two ladies over to the hotel and got them a room. When he got back, Chad was all ready to go look for the coach. Jake jumped on his horse. They followed the road out of town and soon came to the coach. Jake searched around the coach, hoping he would find something. But there was not a thing in sight. Maybe the ladies could tell them.

Chad drove the coach back to town and told the undertaker to take care of the dead men. Jake went up to the room where the ladies were staying. Millie answered the door. "Oh, it is you. Come in. What can we do for you? We have told you everything we know."

"I am sorry to have to put you through this, but I was hoping you might have missed something. By the way, my name is Jake North, and I too have had some misfortune like you, so you see, I would like to see these people behind bars."

"Yes, but I don't think there is anything else we can tell you." Just then Jake saw Nancy twisting a black veil.

"Nancy, is that your veil, or is it something you found?" Nancy did not say a word. She just sat there, twisting the veil.

"She has not said anything since the trouble we had."

"Millie, can you describe any of the gang?"

"Mmm ... well, there was one that I can. She was a tall Spanish lady, and she wore black clothes, as if she was in mourning for a loved one. She had a black veil like the one that Nancy has. I remember now, she put a gun to Nancy's side and told her to move over to the seat I was sitting in. That is when the veil got caught in Nancy's arm, and she dragged it with her."

Jake leaned forward and kissed Millie on the cheek. "Thank you very much. You have helped a lot."

Millie touched her cheek. "Oh, you are a nice man." Then she turned a little and started to blush.

"There is one more thing I would like you to do for me. Do you think you could get the veil away from Nancy later and bring it to me?"

"Of course I will, you dear boy."

Monica was just talking to the gang when an Indian appeared at the back door. "Hey, you, what do you want?" she asked.

The Indian said, "The chief sent me. He wants to talk to you."

"Yeah? Tell him I will come later."

"No, not later, now. He will not wait." Monica and Sammy left with the Indian. They also took a packhorse laden with things for the chief.

Chad was in the office when Jake got there. "Oh, and where did you go off to? I turned around and you were gone."

"I had a hunch, and it panned out. The elderly woman that was on the coach told me what the gang looked like. Well, one of them was dressed all in black. She was a tall Spanish lady. Now who do we know that fits that description?"

"Now let me see. Could it be our old friend Monica?" Chad asked.

"Yes, it is, but she is supposed to be dead."

"All I can say is she did not die and is back making trouble again," Chad replied. "Oh, there is one other thing. Millie is bringing me a veil as evidence." No sooner did he say that than Millie walked in with the veil.

"Mr. North, you asked me to get this for you. I don't know how it will help you, but here."

"Oh, thank you, lovely lady, this will help a lot."

Nigel and Rodney were getting a bit restless. "Nigel, I had enough of sitting around here. What do you say we do something of our own?"

"Yeah, come on. I have just the kind of fun you will like."

The first stop for them was to get some bottles of whiskey. Nigel took Rodney to a small farm just outside of town. They found themselves some bushes to hide behind and waited.

"Nigel, what are we doing here, sitting behind these goddamn bushes?"

"Um, you will see. Just wait."

Just then two beautiful young ladies came out of the house and into the barn.

When Monica got to the Indian camp, they were taken straight to the chief. "Monica, old friend, what do you have for me today?"

Some of the braves started to unpack the packhorse. Monica did not like the way the chief was acting.

Chad wanted to go back out to where the coach was attacked. "What do you hope to find out there?" Jake could not understand Chad's motives."

"The undertaker told me that one of the men was attacked with a knife to the heart. There is only one that I know of that can be that deadly with a knife, so I am hoping that maybe she did not retrieve the knife and it is still out there."

Nigel and Rodney followed them into the barn. "Hi, ladies, want to have a drink with us?" Nigel held up a bottle of whiskey. The two ladies backed off farther into the barn. "Ah, we've come just to be friendly. What are your names?" Rodney held out a bottle of whiskey, as well."

Our names are Beth and Edith, and you will let us pass." Both ladies held their skirt up a bit and started to try to run past them, but it was no use. The men grabbed them as they tried to pass. The ladies screamed and called for help, but their screams fell on deaf ears.

The ladies were not going to give the men what they wanted. Nigel and Rodney knew this, so they just took what they wanted. They ripped at the ladies clothes. But one of the ladies got away and ran up into the loft. She did not see the open doorway where they lowered the bales of hay.

When Chad and Jake got to the area where the attack took place, they started to search the grounds. Chad kicked something, and it sounded like metal. "Here, Jake, I have something," Chad called out.

When they had a good look at it, they could see that it was a very fancy knife. "Yeah, this knife looks as if it is one of a kind," Jake said. Then they looked at it a bit more and saw that it had letters in gold on it.

Beth lost her footing and fell to the ground. They all ran outside. "Hey, Nigel, she may be dead."

"Ah, don't be silly. That was not much of a fall."

Rodney still had hold of Edith. "Where do you think you are going? Come back here." He dragged her back into the barn. He had not finished with her yet.

"No, my friend, I must go to her. Let me go."

"Nope, not yet." Rodney got Edith down on the floor and tore away her dress. He loved to see her naked body. Rodney was getting so excited, he just raped her while she screamed. When Rodney had done what he wanted, he just rolled off to one side. Edith lay there for a while, and then she saw a knife in his belt. She grabbed it and tried to stab him. Rodney was so fast, he took the knife from her and stabbed her instead.

Nigel came into the barn. "Pal, she is dead. We better get out of here."

"Yeah, so is this bitch."


Shana was out riding when she met up with Rodney and Nigel. "What are you two doing out here?"

"Um, the same as you—nothing," Nigel told her.

"Well, we might as well do it together."

"Yeah, that sounds good."

Rodney rode on. As they did not know just where they were going, they kept on going until they came to a big two-story house. They just sat on their horses for a moment, and then Shana said, "Let's go and see if anyone lives there."

When they got to the house, Monica came out. "Hi, how did you find this place?" she asked.

"Monica, we did not know you lived here. Why did you not tell us about this place?" Shana asked.

"I was going to. I just got it back. Come in, and I will fill you all in."

After Monica told them her story, she told Sammy that there were only two ways in—one through the tunnel and one through the swamp. "Sammy, there must be another way of finding this place. Find it, and close the trail that leads into here. The path through the mountains is closed. The Indians will guard the tunnel, and no one comes though the swamp."


Back at the sheriff's office, Chad and Jake continued examining the knife with the gold writing on it, which seemed to be in Spanish.

"I think we will have to get someone to tell us just what this means," Chad said.

Jake was taking a rest and sitting on the porch of the jail when he saw someone loading a packhorse with some things from the house. "Hey, Chad, it looks like someone is moving out of the house at the end of the street," Jake called out.

"Oh, I didn't know anyone was living there," Chad remarked.

Jake wanted to know who was living there, so he went to ask the man who was working there. "Hey, pal, can you tell me who was living here?"

"Sorry, I was just told to take the stuff to another place, and someone will meet us."

Mary and Josh Hiller came home to a horrible sight; both of their daughters murdered. After Josh buried their daughters, he and Mary went to town to see the sheriff. "Sheriff, you must do something about these murders. Our two daughters were murdered."

"Now calm yourself and tell me what happened."

"What is there to tell? One daughter fell from the hayloft, and the other was stabbed to death. But both of them were raped, as well."

"Mr. Hiller, we have had a massive number of killings over the last few weeks." Chad went to him and put his arm around Josh's shoulders. "I am sorry for your loss. But we will find the killers. We promise you."

Jake deiced to take a trip on his own. He thought he would follow the man who was leaving town to meet someone. Jake had a hunch, as usual. But the man was Nigel, and he got wise to the fact that he had a tail. Nigel took Jake on a fool's errand. When Nigel had a chance, he hid the packhorse in some high rocks and then went back to where Jake was coming.

"Stop right there," Nigel called out from behind a large boulder. Jake stopped dead in his tracks with his gun in hand. He sprang off his horse and landed on his feet like a cat. Jake quickly moved behind some boulder and waited. Then Nigel shot at him, and Jake had no choice but to fire back. The shooting went on for some time without anyone getting hurt.

Mr. Hiller left the office. He took his wife to the hotel for a rest before heading for home.

Chad wondered where Jake went off to. Chad was feeling helpless, knowing he could do nothing. He had no leads to go on.

Nigel was taking too long to get back the things, so Monica sent Shana after him. She also sent an Indian to show Shana the way through the tunnel. After Shana got through the tunnel, it did not take her long to find Nigel. She could hear the gunfire from a long way off.

Chad thought that Jake had been gone a long time. *Come on, Chad, old boy, where is your backbone? Move your sorry ass and go find Jake,* Chad told himself. Chad had a fair idea about which way he might have gone.

Shana came up behind Nigel and very quietly asked him, "Hey, what on earth are you doing?"
Nigel turned to see who it was behind him. "I am trying to get rid of this nosy parker."
Shana took a look at just what was what. "I will take care of him. Get ready to move when I give you the nod."

Chad, of course, went the wrong way and ended up at the back of Nigel's packhorse. He untied the horse and slapped it on the rump, and the horse took off fast.

# CHAPTER 5

# So Close But So Far

But the noise of the packhorse running made Nigel scream. "Blast, there is someone up there, and now all of our goods are gone."

"Oh, stop your whining, and get up. We are on the move." Shana stood up and at the same time threw her knife at Jake.

"Oh, damn, I have been stabbed. Chad, are you out there?"

"Yeah, pal, I am on my way. Stay there."

Shana made her getaway and took him back to Monica. "I don't want to be in your shoes when you approach Monica." Shana laughed.

Shana and Nigel slowly walked into the house. "Okay, where are my things, Nigel? Come on, you better have a good answer." Monica was very angry, as she had already been informed of what happened.

"I ... am sorry, but the packhorse got away. I tried to stop him, but I was set upon by the law and had to fight my way out."

Monica brought her hand up, and it went right across Nigel's face. Nigel put his hand up to his face and then turned away. He left the room and sat on the steps. *That bitch will get hers one day. Count on it,* he thought to himself.

The next day an Indian came to the house with the runaway horse.

Monica wanted to take a ride by herself, and when she got to the barn there was the packhorse all intact. "Sammy! Sammy!" she called.

"Yeah, Monica, I am coming. What seems to be the trouble?"

"Um, no trouble. Just how did this horse get here?"

"I don't know. Maybe an Indian found it and brought it in."

"Ah, yes, the chief said he would help me, and he has."

Chad got Jake back to town, and the doctor took care of his arm. "Jake, you were lucky she was not on her game, or you might be dead."

"Yeah, thanks, pal, but take a look at the knife. It is the same as the other one," Jake pointed out.

"That's right, so this means that she is one of a gang that has been terrorizing people." Chad patted Jake on the back. "Good work. Did you get a good look at her?" Chad hoped.

"Sorry, no, but you've seen her too."

"Yeah, but she was too damn quick. Ah, we are no closer in catching them than we were a month ago." Chad sank back into a high-back chair.

"Not quite. We have a fair idea of what she looks like. I am sure if our paths cross again, I will know her." Jake was feeling good about this.

Jake and Chad had to try to find another lead, and that meant going over old ground. Chad had an idea. "Jake, what if we were to trace the old track that we did when we were looking for Monica before?" Chad asked

"Yeah, that is worth a go. We don't have anything else. Let's do it."

The old house would be the first place the law would look for them. "Sammy, I think we will have to change the way we come and go."

"Oh, I don't think that will be necessary, do you?" Sammy did not need the extra work.

"Yes, I do. The law knows the way through the tunnel. You don't think for one moment that a couple of guards are going to stop them. I think we should open up the path through the hill, and get some Indians to help you. I want this done right away," Monica told him.

Chad and Jake did not know that there was work going on to stop them. While Jake and Chad were out of town, Shana wanted to have some fun on her own. She knew there was always a card game going on at the saloon. She walked straight up to the table where it was and said, "Is this a private game, or can anyone join in?"

They all looked at Shana, and then one of them said, "Lady, your money is as good as ours."

Chad and Jake got to the waterfall. "I think we could rest here for the night and get an early start in the morning," Chad suggested.

Sammy and the men worked all night, closing the tunnel. The next step was to open the path through the hills.

Shana was having a winning night until one of the players accused her of cheating. "I saw you deal from the bottom of the deck."

"You did not. I do not cheat."

"I saw her. I say she is cheating. Look at how she keeps on winning." The player got so angry he stood up and turned the table over. All of the other players just walked away. They knew that there was going to be a fight.

Shana stepped back. "If anyone is cheating, it is you. Roll up your sleeve."

"I don't have to, and you cannot make me."

That is when Shana had her knife out very fast. "Maybe this will make you."

After he saw this, he pulled his sleeve up fast, and two aces fell to the floor. Shana walked past the players and went to the hotel.

The other players got hold of the cheat and took him over to the jail. "Here, Deputy, put this cheat behind bars for the judge when he comes." The deputy knew that it would be a long time before the judge came.

"Bert, I am going to let you out if you promise to go straight home and come back when the judge gets here." Bert agreed and then left. But this was not the end of it. He was still reeling from Shana shaming him in public.

The next day Chad and Jake started for the tunnel, but when they got there they were surprised. "Oh, hell, Jake, this damn tunnel is blocked off."

"The bastards. It is happening again. She is one step ahead of us. Now we must find another way around. They will have to have a way in and out."

"Yeah, but where? We can't hang around here and wait for someone to come pass," Chad complained.

Nigel was getting tired of just sitting around. He decided to go it alone. He had been watching the bank for days and knew when a large shipment of money was to be going out to the bigger bank in the east.

The time was right. The bank was taking the money to the depot for the train. Nigel was just leaving the house when Monica stopped him. "Where are you going?" she asked in an angry tone. They were still at odds about the last incident.

"I am tired of just doing nothing, so I am going for a ride, if that is okay with you."

"Don't be a smart mouth. You can keep on riding if that is what you want."

With that, Nigel knew just where he stood and who was getting the blame for whatever happened from now on.

An Indian came to the hotel as Shana was coming. "Miss Shana, I have been sent to take you home."

Chad and Jake had just gotten back to town when Shana and the Indian were leaving. "Chad, that woman on the horse that passed us is the same one that stabbed me."

"Come on. Then we can follow them, and we will find the way to Monica."

Nigel saw them leave and thought this would be a good time to board the train.

It took Shana and the Indian a long time to get to the path through the hills. It was so far. They had to stop and make camp for the night. Chad and Jake stayed back as far as they could and bed down for the night.

Nigel was waiting for the right time to strike. He had put his horse on the special car for horses so he could have a way of getting away. There were two guards on the train and the guards from the bank. Nigel had to figure out a way to get past them. And then it came to him—some sort of distraction. That was when fortune smiled on him. A woman on the train was about to give birth to her first baby. Nigel was sitting next to her, and she started to get contractions. She looked like she was in a great deal of pain.

Nigel jumped up and pulled the cord to stop the train. Both train guards came in. "Okay, who stopped the train, and why?" one guard asked.

"I did," Nigel said.

The woman gave out an almighty scream. Then the guards got all the answers. Nigel was told to step out of the way. This gave him the reason to leave the train and walk to the baggage car.

Nigel banged on the door and shouted out, "You are needed up front."

The door flung open. "What the hell for?" one of the guards asked, but as he did Nigel shot him in the face, and he fell to the ground. Before the other one could shut the door, he was shot too. He fell on the floor of the car.

With some dynamite Nigel blew open the door of the safe, grabbed the two bank bags, and then left a note saying "Thanks, Monica." He then jumped down, got his horse, and headed for the border.

As soon as the lady was ready to travel again, the train went on to the next station. This was only a whistle stop, so they had to get some wagons to take all of the passengers back to town. When the deputy heard about the trouble, all he could do was send a messenger to Chad.

Chad and Jake followed Shana and the Indian to the new path through the hills.

It took the messenger a long time to find Chad, and by this time Chad and Jake had found Monica's home. But they also found some braves with spears pointed at them. "Gee, I hate this. Every time we come here we have spears poking us in the back," Jake said.

"Yeah, but this time we'll lose, so be ready to move when I give you the nod," Chad told him. Chad stood his ground and did not move when the Indian told them to. But suddenly Chad did move. That was when Jake moved back a bit, grabbed one of the spears, and flung the Indian around until he was taken off his feet. That was when Jake and Chad quickly jumped back on their horses and rode back through the path.

At the waterfall they met up with the messenger. He told Chad all about the train robbery. "Jake, we better get back to town. We have more things to worry about. We will come back to this later."

Nigel found himself a nice little cave in which he could hole up in for now.

The people of Mexico did not like strangers coming. They called them gringos.

The townspeople rallied around the wagons when they came into town. They made sure they had all the help they needed.

As soon as Chad got back to the office, the deputy said, "Oh, finally, where the hell have you been? I have been run off my feet with people wanting help."

"Well, now you can take a rest. I will handle things."

The stationmaster came into the office. "Sheriff, we found this note left in the safe. It may be a lead."

"Thank you. Every little bit helps right now." Chad read the note and then handed it to Jake. "What do you think it means?"

Jake shook his head. "I don't know. 'Thanks, Monica.' It could mean that Monica is getting smart, or it could be someone else who did the robbery and is trying to put the blame on Monica."

"Jake, I cannot see Monica leaving a note. She never has before. I am inclined to go with someone else did the robbery and is trying to shift the blame."

"I think you are right."

# CHAPTER 6

# Change of Mind

Nigel was sound asleep when a young Mexican girl came in, looking for her runaway goat. "Senor, wake up. What are you doing here? You cannot sleep here. You will catch your death from a cold."

Nigel awoke. "Who the hell is that? Go away, and leave me alone," he moaned.

"No, senor, I will take you to my home. Come, you get up." She tugged at his shirt. "Get up."

Nigel got up and said, "All right, you win. I will come home with you." He had already hid the two bags of money.

Monica had heard about the train robbery and how someone had been laying blame on her. She wanted to find Nigel and make him part with some of the money. If she was going to be blamed, they might as well have some of the glory.

"Monica, what makes you so sure it was Nigel?" Sammy asked.

"Oh, I am sure because we had a falling out and this is his way of getting even. Now I want everyone to keep an eye out for him."

"I think I know just where he might be."

"Shana, where do you think he might be holed up?" Monica was anxious to find out where he was, but Shana was not about to give anything away. She wanted him for herself, and she wanted all the money.

Chad and Jake went back over old ground to try to get some kind of lead. "Chad, we know the way into Monica's home, but we will have to be careful. You know they have guards."

"Yeah, that's right."

When they got to the path, they left their horses and went on foot, all the time keeping out of sight so they could get the drop on the guards.

Shana had packed up her horse and left the house. But she did not expect to run into the law. She was like Monica. With a sixth sense, she knew there were someone up ahead.

Chad heard someone or something. "Jake, did you hear that?"
"No, what?"
"Quiet, you will hear it."
They both sat there, and then they heard it again. "Yeah, someone is up ahead," Jake said. There was not much cover on the path—mainly rocks and high cliffs. But they were able to find some very large rocks to get behind.

The Mexican girl, Anna, had given Nigel something to drink. "Now you will sleep for a while. You will need it." When Nigel was fast asleep, Anna went back to the cave and looked to see if any of Nigel's things were around. She found a jacket, and when she lifted it up she made some stones move a bit. That was when she saw the money bags. Anna was a very smart girl. She took the bags, tied them with some rope, and pulled the rope high up into a tree.

Shana had to get out of the path somehow, so she thought of taking a track up the side of the cliff. It meant walking her horse and climbing a little higher. Soon she came down at the back of the law and then kept on going. Shana did not want to get into a shooting war; she had more important things to worry about.

Chad and Jake thought the trouble had passed, but how? That was not all they had to think about; they still had to get past the guards.
There were two guards up high, one on each side of the cliffs. "Do you have any idea how we are going to get past them?" Chad asked.

"Well, as a matter of fact, I do, but you may not like it."

"Ah, don't tell me it involves climbing."

"You got it. Yes, it is the only way we are going to get past those two."

So the climbing began. Jake slipped up behind one Indian, slit his throat, and then came back down. As Jake was doing that, Chad had his Indian done too.

This gave way to both of them entering the area without being spotted. The first place they checked out was the barn They knew this place well—maybe too well.

The barn brought back some awful memories for them. They just started to search, when Monica came into the barn. They had to duck for cover. Monica had the uneasy feeling that she was being watched. She left the barn in a hurry and sent an Indian servant out to take a look.

"Phew, that was close! So she is alive and well," Chad said.

"Yeah, and that sent cold shivers up my spine." Jake went back to searching, and they did not see the Indian. With a gun in his hand, he said, "You come out of there, or I will shoot."

This took them by surprise. "You will go to the house. Miss Monica will know what to do with you."

Anna waited till Nigel woke up. Then she said, "Nigel, I found your jacket, and I also found something else. Tell me, did you rob the train?"

"Oh, you found that, did you? Where is it?"

"It is safe for now. You will give it back, yes?"

"No, well, not yet. I want someone to pay big-time for this robbery.

"Nigel, that is not right. You did the robbery. You must turn yourself in and give back the money."

Nigel needed some time to think about what Anna said to him. Maybe this could work for him.

Anna could see that Nigel had to have some time so she went. There was work to do. Nigel offered to help her with the work. Maybe Nigel was looking for a way to turn his life around.

Shana was not far from the border, and was in a hurry to get her hands on Nigel's throat. She rode hard and fast, and soon she got to the cave that they both knew about.

Chad and Jake were taken to Monica, who was sitting in a big armchair. The Indian pushed the two of them down to the floor near her feet.

"Well, well, we meet again. How long has it been? Come, come, boys, don't be shy. You are among friends here." She laughed, and Jake and Chad got to their feet.

"You might have the upper hand now, but it won't last. You know it did not last long the last time you held us captive," Chad told her.

"Oh, you have some backup out there, have you? Well, they won't be out there long this time. You see, we have friends here now." Monica walked around the two of them. This time she was carrying a whip with her. Monica cracked the whip next to Jake's feet. "You know I should have made sure there was no one left when I killed all of your family."

This made Jake angry enough to grab the end of the whip. Monica tried to pull it back, but Jake had a good grip on it. He tugged hard, and then she fell to the floor. While Jake was busy with her, Chad made sure that no one interfered. Jake had Monica all tied up with the whip. But in order to get away, they had to let her go. So they sat her down on a chair and found something to tie her up with. Chad grabbed the cord from around the drapes. Now it was time for them to slip out the back.

After they got far enough away, Jake asked, "Hey, why did you let her go? We had her just where we wanted her."

"Think about it. We don't have any proof that she had anything to do with the last robbery or any of the others."

"Yes, I understand that, but she is a fugitive from justice."

"I know that, but all the proof we had on that time was lost in the hotel fire. So we have nothing." Jake did not like what he heard, but there was nothing he could do.

Shana found him working in the fields with a Mexican lady. She could not believe her eyes. As soon as she got a chance, she got a hold of Nigel and dragged him into a nearby barn. "What do you think you are playing? You better tell me where the money is."

Nigel tried to get out of Shana's grip, but she was too strong for him. "Let me go or you will get nothing," Nigel yelled.

"No, you little worm, spill it or you are dead meat."

"Oh, that would be smart. Then you will get nothing."

Shana knew she had no choice but to let him go. As soon as he got free, he ran just like a scared rabbit.

Rodney and Sammy had been away, but when they got back they found Monica tied up to a chair. "About time you two got back. Get me out of this," she yelled.

Sammy untied Monica, and they went straight upstairs to talk. Rodney did not like being left out of the talks. This sort of thing happened once too often, so he decided to leave. It looked like they did not need anyone but each other.

This meant that the gang was splitting up, but he was going to get even with them. Monica came downstairs and found that Rodney was not there. She called out to Sammy, "Sammy, check Rodney's room. I think he is a runner."

Sammy came downstairs. "You're right. All of his things are gone." Monica knew there was trouble in the wind. Once more she had to leave her home and go underground.

It was a long way back to town, so Jake and Chad thought they should rest the horses for the night. "Jake, now that we know the way to Monica's house, I was thinking she may pull up stakes."

"You know, I had the same thought. Maybe we should hang around for a bit and see if she makes a move."

Monica was going to make a move, but she was going to make sure that there were no prying eyes. She had to get rid of all of the evidence to show that she was ever there. Monica sent Sammy to find her somewhere to live, somewhere that no one would find them in a hurry.

Chad and Jake moved farther onto the path and just out of sight of the guards. But they could still see Monica's house and what she was doing.

As Far as Rodney was concerned, the gang was over, and it was time to get lost. Rodney found himself going through the swamp. He had friends on the other side of the swamp. It was not the best place, but it would do until he could find somewhere else to go.

Nigel ran to Anna's house. "Anna, you must tell me where you hid the money," he begged.

"Nigel, are you going to give it back?"

"Yes, it's not worth risking my life for. I have a life here, but this means that I will have to turn myself in."

"You know you are doing the right thing. I will be here when it is all over. You know I love you a lot, and no matter how long it takes I will wait."

Anna gave Nigel the bags, and after he said good-bye he set out to go back across the border.

Shana was waiting for Nigel to leave so she could follow him. The road Nigel took led right back to town. Shana did not like this. She hoped he would go to Monica's. What Shana did not know was that Monica was moving to a new place. Nigel knew it was a very long way to town, so he stopped for the night. Shana stayed back out of sight and settled down for the night.

Rodney found his friends. "Hey, Harry, can I stay with you for a while?"

"What do you mean, Rodney? Until the heat is off, there is no place for you. We have all changed. We do not have the law after us anymore."

Rodney did not know what to say except "Well, I will have to find somewhere else. Nice friend you turned out to be, after all we have been to each other. Have you forgotten we had a lot of fun?"

"Those days are over. We don't want any trouble now. Will you go?"

Rodney walked away from his friend's home, but he was very angry. He went past the house, and after lighting a cigarette, he flicked the match into the dry grass near the house. Everything went up in flames. "Now where are you going to live, pal?"

Everything was going wrong for all of the gang. Monica and Sammy had to move on. Shana was tailing Nigel. Chad and Jake were watching to see what was going to happen.

The sun came up the next day—a brand-new day—and Nigel got started. He thought he could still get Monica blamed for the robbery. He had to think about how he was going to do this. Nigel started for the waterfall, not knowing that the tunnel had been closed. Shana followed him but did not know just what he was doing. He was going in a different direction to the town.

Rodney rode thought the swamp again and came out at the Indian camp. He did not want to get into a war with the Indians, so he went up into the hills. Now he was on his own and had time to think about Sammy and Monica and what he was going to do to get even.

Sammy had found an abandoned house for Monica. After he had taken her there, he then had to go back to the other house. Monica wanted everything burned down to the ground.

Chad saw the flames leap high into the sky. "Jake, look, she has had the place set alight."

"Oh, no, we must stop it. We need to go through the place for evidence."

"Okay, let's get on down there and see what we can save."

As soon as they tried to put out the flames, Sammy was about to set fire to the barn. Chad and Jake returned the fire, and the fight lasted for a while. Sammy thought he was outmatched, so he left.

After they found that Sammy had fled, they went back to searching what was left of the house. Nothing was salvageable that was of any use to them. Now they had to search the barn, and maybe they could come up with something there.

# CHAPTER 7

# The Falling Out

Nigel sat on the riverbank to think about getting even with Monica. Shana came up behind him. "What the bloody hell do you think you are doing? Where is the money? You know, we were friends once. We could be again if you are willing to share the money."

Rodney was roaming all over the place, sleeping wherever he could. It was not long before he came up to were Shana and Nigel were, and he overheard them talking about some money. "Well, blow me down. Who would have thought I would run into you two!"

They were shocked to see Rodney. "What the hell, you! We never thought we would lay eyes on you again," Shana snarled.

"Yes, well, here I am in the flesh, you might say. Now did I hear someone mention some money?" he asked, standing there with a big grin on his face.

Nigel looked at Shana. "Ah, what money would that be, Rodney? We don't have any money to speak of," he said with a sly look on his face.

"Don't play me for a fool. I know all about the big money you have." Rodney was telling them a lie, but they did not know if he knew or not.

Shana got to Nigel and told him, "I don't trust him, but if you want to give him some of the money, it comes out of your share."

"Just a minute, who said you were getting a share? I am going to hand it in and tell them I found it at Monica's home."

Shana was not happy about this. "No, you are not. I will have some of the money or all of it—it's up to you." Then she put one of her knives to his side.

Nigel had no other choice. "When you put it that way, okay, half of it is yours. Now what do we do about Rodney?"

"You leave him to me. He will not be a problem."

Chad went up into the loft to search, and Jake stayed down where the horses were. They kept on looking and not taking any notice of what Sammy was doing. "Jake, up here I found Monica's strongbox. This is all we need," Chad called out.

Jake went up to help him with the box. Sammy set fire to the front of the barn, and if they were to get out they had to go out through the back wall, where Sammy was waiting for them.

"Blaze, Jake, the place is on fire. We will have to break through the back wall."

"Yeah, pal, that won't be too hard. It is all but rotten through anyway."

Monica did not like waiting for Sammy to return. He had been gone too long, so she set out to look for him. She could see the flames coming from the house, so she knew he had to have been there. When she got closer, she could see that the barn was on fire too.

Chad broke thought the back wall, and as soon as they got out, Sammy was there with his gun pointed straight at them. "Drop the box," he shouted.

Jake had hold of one end, and Chad had the other. "Oh, you want the box? Okay, here it is." They tossed the box right at Sammy's face, and he was out cold. Chad got a small piece of leather, which he always carried, from his back pocket. "Now you will do no more harm."

A shot rang out from behind them, and it took Jake's hat off. They had to quickly find some cover.

"Who the bloody hell is that?" Chad asked.

The voice called out, "Let my friend loose or the next bullet will find its mark." They knew that voice and knew she meant what she said. But there was no way they were going to give up now.

Nigel went to where he had hidden the money, but instead of getting the bags, he got the gun he had hidden there. "This money is going back to the bank." He had them covered with the gun well, as he thought.

"What do you know, the worm has found some guts." With that, Shana flung a knife, and it hit Nigel in the arm. He had to drop the gun. Shana was very quick and took the bags from their hiding place. "Now, Nigel, the shoe is on the other foot, so to speak."

Nigel was rolling on the ground in pain. "Take the damn money. It has caused me nothing but trouble."

Rodney was not going to leave it all up to Shana, with his gun pointed right at Shana's heart. "Not so fast, Shana. Half of that is mine, so drop one bag."

Shana was not taking any chances, so she dropped one bag and then left in a hurry. She was not hanging around for more arguments. Nigel was left to take care of himself. As soon as he had patched himself up, he took off after the two of them. They would not have time to use any of the money.

Monica was not going to wait for them to make up their minds, so she fired a shot. It hit Chad in the side. "Ah, you bitch, now it will get even harder for you to get your friend free." With that, Chad fired back. Jake dragged Chad and the box around to the other side of the barn. He went back for Sammy, who was still unconscious, got him by the shirt collar, and dragged him back too.

The flames of the burning barn gave them good cover, so they could get to the horses.

Jake bundled Sammy across his saddle and tied him there. He then helped Chad to his horse. As it was getting late, Jake found a safe behind some rocks halfway up the path. Chad had gotten his bandanna from around his neck and stuffed it under his shirt.

Sammy started to stir. "What hit me? Oh, my head! Where are we?"

Jake thought it would be better if he got Sammy down off his horse. Jake sat Sammy down next to Chad. His hands and feet were still tied up. There was no way he was getting loose.

Monica had failed in her attempt to free Sammy, and this made her very angry. She made a beeline for the Indians for help. But when she got to the Indian camp, it was not there. They had pulled up stakes. There was one thing left. There were a pile of stones and a message that read, "We don't help white eyes anymore. Too much trouble with the soldiers coming from fort."

Monica was so angry she could have bitten the head off a rattlesnake. After she had rested a night, she then thought she would take matters into her own hands.

Having all of her gang gone, one way or the other she knew she was on her own again. Back at the new place that Sammy had found for her, she sat alone and started to drink whiskey. This was something she had never done before.

Shana and Rodney were just getting to the path, and Shana, who was a very greedy woman, was thinking of a way to get all of the money before they got to the path. Nigel had gotten very close to them and decided to hang back until he could get to a good place to attack them.

The path had a lot of very high mountainsides, and it had a lot of tracks winding in and around. Jake knew the tracks and where to find them. He got Sammy onto his horse again and helped Chad with his. "Chad, I am going to go up high around the path. Do you think you will make it with your bad side?"

"Yeah, pal, I will make it. Don't you worry about that."

"Yeah, what about me? You have me hog-tied to this here animal. If he loses his footing, I am a goner," Sammy complain.

"You will just have to make sure that he does not," Jake barked back at him.

After Monica had gotten herself good and drunk, she decided to go to the path. There was nothing more dangerous than a drunk woman.

Shana saw the perfect place to let Rodney have it. There was a water hole up the path a bit. "Hey, Rodney, there is a water hole up a ways. We need some water. Will you get it? I want to fix my saddle. It has come lose," she said in a nice tone.

"Yeah, okay, I won't be long. We don't want to stay here too long. It is not safe."

*Oh, you don't know how true that is,* she said to herself.

As soon as Rodney bent down to get the water, she had one of her knives out and slit his throat. Blood poured everywhere. Now she had all the money and hightailed out of there.

As Nigel was not far from them, he had seen everything she did. There was a secret place that Nigel and Shana both knew about. They both thought alike. That was because they were sister and brother. The place was the family home before their mother and father died.

Monica was halfway along the path. She was so drunk, she fell off her horse. Monica did not care. She just lay there and laughed out loud. Nigel got to Monica first and could tell she was in a bad way. "Hey, Monica, are you all right?" he asked her.

Monica had one eye closed, but she looked up at Nigel. "Who the devil are you? Tell me now or I will shoot you." Monica pulled out her gun and waved it around.

"Now, Monica, don't be silly. That thing could go off at any time. Please put it down."

"What will you do, take it away from me? You are nothing but a pantywaist. You could not harm anyone. Ha-ha." She kept on waving the gun around.

Shana was ahead of all that was going on, and then suddenly she heard a shot. She heard some screaming, which made her turn around and go back. Shana had a bad feeling in the pit of her stomach that something had happened.

When Shana got back to where Nigel and Monica were, she found both of them lying on the ground facedown. She got a hold of Nigel and turned him over. He had a gunshot wound in the shoulder, but he was still. Shana sat him up. "Nigel, come on, wake up. I will get you home."

"Oh, what happen?" Then he put his hand up to his shoulder, and when he took it away it was covered in blood. "Mmm, that hurts. Oh, so much pain. Any more of this and I will be dead."

"Steady up, you have a small wound in the shoulder. Get a grip, brother." She whacked him on the head.

Chad and Jake were on their way down the hillside with Sammy in tow. They had not seen Monica or any of the others. If they had that would have been too much for them to handle. Sammy was making things hard enough.

Monica had sobered up and was asking, "What are you two doing, and who shot me in the side?" She was so angry.

"You were so off your face. You have been drinking. I tried to take the gun away from you, but you argued with me," Nigel told her. "Come on, Monica, we will help you to get home." They had to help her. They did not want her to get wind of the money they had.

Chad and Jake got back to town, and Sammy was put into one of the cells. "Hey, Sheriff, I am hurting here. I need a doctor."

"What the hell do you need a doctor for? You might have a bad headache. When I see the doctor I will get you something for it. Now shut up." Chad waited for the doctor to come across the street.

Some soldiers came to the office. "Where can I find the sheriff?" the captain asked.

"I am the sheriff. What can I do for you?" Chad hobbled to the captain.

"Oh, I am sorry, I did not know you were injured. We have a dead man out here. We found him up the path. He had his throat slit."

"Oh, you better take him over to the undertaker down the street. How is it that you found him?"

"We were out on patrol. We have to keep the Indians in check."

Just as the captain was leaving, Jake and the doctor came back. After the doctor had finished, he said, "The bullet is, but you must rest for a few days."

Jake was looking though the strongbox they had found at Monica's place. "What do we have there, Jake?"

"Oh, it is laden with lots of good things that will put Monica away for a very long time."

Chad was feeling good about what he had just heard. With all of the trouble they had gone through, they finally had some good news for a change.

Shana and Nigel got Monica home. What she did not know was that the house that Sammy found abandoned was Nigel and Shana's family home. Shana took Nigel outside after settling Monica in. "Nigel, we better not tell Monica that this is our home. We know all about this place, and we should keep it that way."

"Yeah, I guess you are right, but where did you put the money?"

"Ah, little brother, you don't need to know that right now. I will let you know when the time is right."

Nigel went to make sure the horses were fed, and he looked around for the money. He was not going to trust Shana. He knew her too well. She had a dark side to her.

Shana got some whiskey and a sharp knife, and she was going to work on Monica's side where she took a bullet.

"What do you think you are going to do with that?" Monica screamed.

"I have to remove that bullet from your side. We cannot risk getting a doctor to you."

"I hope you know what you are doing, my girl."

Shana called Nigel in to hold Monica down while she got the bullet out. Halfway through it all, Monica passed out, and that made things a lot easier. When they finished, they left her to rest. It was the next day before Monica woke up and started to scream. "What the bloody hell have you bastards done to me?"

Shana was getting tired of playing nursemaid to Monica and all of her screaming. "Hold your horses, Monica, I am coming. You were shot in the side, and I fixed you up. Don't try to move. You have to stay put for a couple of days. Oh, don't bother thanking me." Shana just stood there, looking at Monica's wound.

"It seems you know your stuff. Thank you."

Sammy was making noises in his cell. He wanted to get out. Jake yelled at him, "Keep that up and you won't live to see the judge."

"Yeah, when do I get something to eat?"

"Your food is on the way over. I cannot make it get here any faster, so shut up."

A young girl from the hotel came to the jail with a tray laden with food.

It took a few days before Monica was up and about. She propped herself up in a big chair. "Now, I have seen you walk around, talking to yourself about some kind of secret. Do not make the mistake of thinking I am a dummy. You better come clean now, and it won't go hard on you if I find out later," Monica promised.

"If you think we are going to tell you anything, you're the one that is stupid." Monica did not like what she was told. Shana walked around Monica, knowing she had the upper hand.

Nigel was outside, still looking for the money. It was driving him mad. He wanted to get rid of the money. He knew he had searched all over the place except inside.

# CHAPTER 8

# The End Is Near

Chad was starting to move about a bit. He went to the cell that Sammy was in. "Sammy, you know if you tell me all I want to know, I could talk to the judge for you. He might go easy on you."

"I will tell you nothing," Sammy snarled.

"Suit yourself, but at the moment you are facing the hangman's rope. There is not much I can do to help you."

Sammy sank back down on his bed and thought about what Chad had told him. He was sure he did not want to be hanged, not for anybody.

Monica was sitting there, watching Nigel clean his gun. "Hey, pantywaist, are you thinking of using that thing? You should watch out, you might shoot your foot. Ha-ha." She laughed.

"Shut your big mouth, woman. I am not in the mood for your smart mouth," Nigel snapped.

Monica walked outside to the barn to see that her horse was all right. Shana was in the barn, sharpening her knives. "It looks like you two are expecting a war. What is it between you two? Are you two lovers or what?"

"Monica, I think it is about time I told you something. You never took the time to find out about the people you run with."

"No, I trust in what I see, and I am usually a good judge of people when I meet them. Why are you bringing this up now?" Monica wondered what Shana was up to.

Sammy called out to Chad. "Hey, Sheriff, I want to talk to you. I am not hanging for anyone."

"Okay, I will get someone to write this down."

Chad told Jake that Sammy was going to talk. This was a big break. They never had it like this before.

Once Sammy got going, there was no stopping him. What he said was in the strongbox helped a lot.

While Monica was outside talking to Shana, Nigel looked in Shana's bedroom. He had all but given up when he walked on one of the floorboards and it cracked a bit. Nigel moved the board and found what he was looking for. He quickly dragged the two bags out and returned the board so it looked like it had never been moved. Now all he had to do was to hide the bags so Shana would not find them.

The next day the judge came into town. As soon as he was settled, Chad visited the judge in his room at the hotel. After telling the judge all about Sammy and how he had come clean and confessed, the judge set his trial for the next day.

Monica was surprised to hear that Nigel and Shana were brother and sister. "Well, you hid that. Why didn't you tell me? Is it because you did not trust me or something?" Monica asked.

"Not at first, and then the time was not right, so we just thought it was better to not tell anyone." Shana just walked away.

Shana did not tell her that the house had been theirs. She was not going to tell her all of it. Nigel came out on the porch and sat down on the step. Shana wondered what he had been up to. He had that look on his face. She always knew when Nigel was up to something. "What have you been up to, monkey? Don't try to lie to me. I know when you lie," Shana said, looking straight at him.

"You think you are so smart, don't you? Well, you are wrong this time." He looked right back at her.

Monica came over to the two of them and told them she was planning another job. "Do you two want in on this, or will Sammy and I do it alone? By the way, we have to get Sammy out of jail first."

"Um, how do you think we are going to do this?" Nigel asked.

"I hope you have a super plan. It won't be easy," Shana snarled.

"I do have a plan, but I can also see that you are not interested in getting my good friend out of jail."

After Sammy told the judge all he knew about the rest of the gang, the judge could see that Sammy was guilty of aiding and abetting, and he sentenced him to one year in prison.

Both Chad and Jake were glad that someone was taken off the streets for a while. Now they would set things in motion to get the others as soon as they could.

Chad and Jake were in the office, talking about transporting Sammy to the prison. "You know that when we do, there will be someone there to try to free him," Jake said.

"You can count on that. We will have to have the prison wagon guarded with extra guns, man."

The road the wagon was to take was quite open most of the way, but there was a blind spot. It had a lot of trees and rocks near the road, which was a very good place for an ambush.

No one knew, but Monica was in the courtroom when Sammy was sentenced. She had a very good disguise, and no one even knew who she was. Chad kept on looking at her, but he could not make the pieces fit. "Hey, Jake, did you notice that lady at the back of the courtroom? I have the feeling that I know her."

"Funny, I have the same feeling. Hey, could it be Monica?" Jake asked.

"You mean she had the nerve to come that close?" Chad replied.

Monica told Shana and Nigel just how she planned to get Sammy.

"Monica, you know he spilled his guts and told them all about us. I, for one, will not be helping you to free that rat."

"Things have changed in that direction. I am only going to get even. You know what I mean."

"Yes, indeed I do. In that case I will help you," Shana assured her.

The day came when they had to take Sammy to prison. Sammy was handcuffed and led out to the wagon. All of the armed men where already on top of the wagon, and one was alongside the driver. Monica had her people in place, waiting for the wagon to come by.

But what they did not know was that Chad had changed the route at the last minute. Monica and her people sat out there until the sun was high in the sky. "Damn, blast, the rotten mongrels changed the route on us. They will pay big for this," she screamed.

Nigel thought it was a good time to plant the bags of money on Monica. He knew that when she calmed down she would go after the bank.

Shana had all she could take. Everything was going wrong, and she just had to get away for a while. There was a lake near the house where her father took her and Nigel fishing sometimes. Shana headed for it with her pole and some worms from the garden. This left Nigel and Monica to plan the bank job.

Chad was sitting back in his chair, smiling. "What has you so happy?" Jake asked him.

"Ah, we outsmarted Monica. Sammy is out of her clutches. Now we can concentrate on getting her and the rest of the gang."

Chad smiled. "Well, I can see how that would make you smile, but have you got another smart plan to do that?"

Jake was all out of ideas, and Chad said, "No, not yet, but I will come up with something."

"One step at a time, old boy, as Albert would say."

Bert was on his way to the hotel for another card game. He had to pass the Gomez family home. That was Shana and Nigel's home. Their parents were killed by Indians. When they were out in the field, looking for stray cows, the Indians did not know there were any children. They were only teenagers, but they were old enough to take care of themselves. Bert always walked down by the lake, and he never thought he would see anyone.

Shana was always careful, and when she heard someone coming she ducked behind a large tree. Monica told Nigel that she was going to blow the jail first and then rob the bank. He was only half listening to her; he had his own agenda. Nigel had put the money bags in Monica's saddlebags.

She got the dynamite out and gave it to Nigel. "I want you to put this near the jail. Just make sure that the jail blows up. I will be over at the bank, waiting for it to go up. Then I will walk into the bank and hold it up. Everyone should be outside, looking at the fireworks. Ha-ha, this is too good. I can hardly wait." She walked around, wringing her hands.

At the back of the jail, there were some very large rocks, and that was what Nigel was going to blow up.

Bert saw Shana duck behind the tree with his gun at the ready. He called out, "You, there, come out or I will shoot you."

Shana came out from behind the tree. "Hold your fire. It is me, Bert—Shana. I am just doing some fishing." She thought if she was nice to him he might drop his guard and lower his gun. And he did.

"Little Shana, I have not seen you … ha, let me see … ah, yes, since you flees me at the hotel." He walked a little closer to her and then put his foot behind her leg and tripped her. "I told you that I would get even with you." He grabbed the rope from his horse, and as she had fallen down the bank a bit, he had time to grab her and tie her to the tree behind which she was hiding.

Shana was not sure what Bert had in mind, but she knew it was not going to be good. Bert had not forgotten the terror Shana and Nigel caused him when they were younger. And now it was payback time. "You and your brother caused me and my good wife a lot of pain. Now I am going to cause you a lot of pain."

But first he sat down and had a drink of whiskey. This gave Shana time to get herself out of the fix she was in. Shana had a knife in the top of her boot—if only she could reach it.

When Nigel got to the back of the jail, he had to wait till he saw Monica at the bank.

Chad and Jake were going over the events of the day and did not see Monica ride up lane way to the back of the bank. Nigel got the signal, and he quickly shoved a note under the back door of the jail. Then he banged on the door to make sure that they got the message. Jake went out to see what was going on, and as he bent down to pick up the note, Nigel blew up the rock at the back door. The force of the explosion knocked him back. He fell with a hard thump. "What the hell is going on out there? A man can't think," Chad called, but when his call went unanswered, he went out to the back. "Jake, are you all right?"

Jake handed him the note. "Yeah, here, read this." The note said Monica was robbing the bank, and she had the rail money in her saddlebags too.

Chad helped Jake to a chair. "You stay there. I am going to catch Monica."

"What the hell? You will need my help. She is very cunning."

All was going as Monica said it would. She had the bank manager open the safe. She was in no mood to take any chances, so she shot him. While she was taking the money from the safe, Chad quietly came up behind her, and with his gun in her back she knew it was all but over.

"Ah, let me guess. Chad, right?"

"Come on, Monica, don't make this any harder than it has to be."

At the jail, Chad put Monica in one of the cells. She walked in nice and calm. Jake came in with the two bags of money. "Right where we were told they would be, in her saddlebags." Jake held up the money bags.

Nigel hightailed back home. He wanted to tell Shana about what had just happened, but she was nowhere to be found. Shana was still trying to get herself free. Bert had finished the bottle of whiskey and fell asleep. Shana had one arm free, so she could reach the knife. As soon as she was free, she used the knife on Bert. *No more card game for him,* she thought.

Shana took off for home, leaving poor Bert lying there, bleeding to death. "Nigel, are you home? It is me, Shana."

Nigel came in to see what the fuss was all about.

"There you are. What have you been doing? I was looking for you."

"Oh, nothing, just packing up. I have had enough of this life, so I am out of here."

"Um, Nigel, what did you do with the money bags? I know you found them in my room."

Nigel went up to his sister and put his arm around her shoulders. "Sister, dear, you are not going to like this, but I gave it back."

"What? You are an idiot. I wanted that money. It would have set me up for a long time."

Because Chad never had Monica searched, they did not see the dynamite she had under her dress. As soon as Chad and Jake left the office to talk to the bank manager about the robbery that never happened and to tell him that they had recovered all of the train robbery money, Monica set about setting the dynamite and covering herself with the bed mattress so she did not get hurt. After she lit the fuse, the dynamite blew a hole in the wall of the cell, just big enough for her to crawl through. Chad ran back to the jail. Jake went around the back only to find a gaping hole in the wall. "Come on, Jake, she could not have gotten too far. She did not have a horse. We will catch her easily."

Nigel set out for Mexico, to Anna and a different life, while Shana sat on the porch, feeling let down. But this was not going to set her back for long. When she thought about it, she knew she could help Monica out of jail. Little did she know that Monica got herself out of jail and was headed her way. Shana was not far from town when she saw Monica running. "Hey, Monica, it is me, Shana. I have come to help you," she called out very loud. She called out so loudly that Chad and Jake heard her.

Monica ran back into some bushes, and then she came around behind Shana. "Hey, Shana, over here," she called softly.

Chad and Jake split up; one went around the track, and the other went into the bushes. Monica was grateful that Shana had come to help her, but there was no time for talking. They had to get out of there fast. Both women knew it was the hangman's noose for them if they were taken alive. So Monica and Shana both made a pact not to be taken alive.

It was a long ride, but they soon came to the waterfall. This end of the waterfall was not blocked off. This was a good place to hide.

They knew that the law was not far behind them, so there was no more they could do but dig in and fight it out. Shana went farther into the tunnel, and she saw the hole in the roof of the tunnel. "Monica, we can get out this way." She pointed to the roof.

"Oh, yes, if we can get up there, we might be able to get out."

While they were trying to find a way up to the roof, Chad and Jake got to the riverbank. Jake waded out to the edge of the waterfall, and he could hear them talking. "Chad, they are in here. We have them cornered," Jake called out.

Monica moved to the entrance to the tunnel and started to shoot. One bullet just missed Jake's head. This made him move back a bit.

Chad got his rifle, went down on one knee, and fired off a few shots at Monica. He was a crack shot with the rifle. One bullet grazed Monica's hand. She dropped the gun and moved inside, screaming, "Oh, my hand! Oh, my hand!" She took the bandanna from around her neck and wrapped it around her hand. "That's it. They are not taking me alive."

Monica pushed past Shana. "Let me have a look at that hole. I am going to get up there."

Shana just stood there and said, "Good luck. I could not find a way up. Maybe you will have a better idea," Shana sniped.

Little did they know that Chad and Jake had gotten closer to the entrance. Chad called out, "Come out with your hands up. There is nowhere for you to run."

Shana was not giving up so easily. Monica found a vine that was short and sticking out of the wall of the tunnel. She grabbed it and started to pull on it. The vine came out a little more, just enough for them to get a hold of it and climb up.

Monica was the first one out. She found that it was on top of the waterfall. Shana came up next. They had to take care, as the rocks were slippery. Chad heard them, and when he looked up he could see both of them. "Damn, how the hell did they get up there? If they get across to the other side, there will be no way we can stop them."

Jake took a look and then fired a shot. It did not miss its target. It hit Shana in the side, and she fell.

Monica called out, "Shana! Shana! Oh, you bastard, you killed my very good friend. I hope you rot in hell." Then she jumped to her death. Chad and Jake could do nothing but stand there and watch the two bodies float down the river.

## THE END

This book is part two of *Monica's Outlaws*. As you may know, Monica was badly hurt, but a friend took her to her father's to recover. Her father did all he could. After three long years, Monica recovered from her ordeal. Now she is ready to take her revenge on all of the people who hurt her and took her daughter away from her. Her father thought he could change her, but she was not having any of his nagging about changing.

# ABOUT THE AUTHOR

Patricia has written several books, some for children and some for adults. She lives in a small town called Taree, which is north of New South Wales, Australia. Patricia loves to write. The stories come easily to her. She has a very good imagination, and this helps her a lot.